WALT DISNEY's
Cinderella

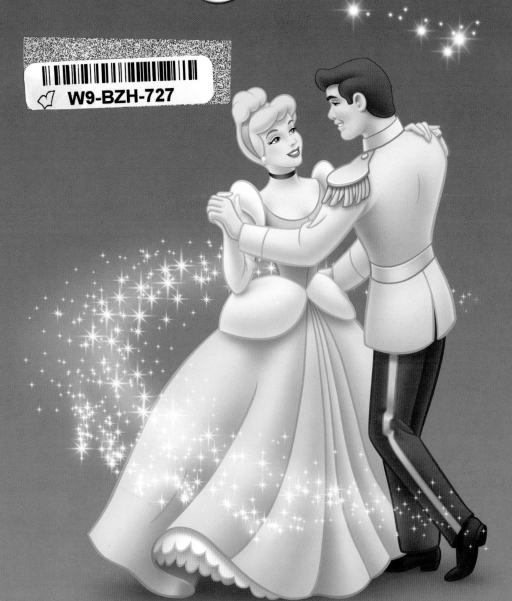

Have an adult help you remove the perforated sticker pages.

Random House New York

Copyright © 2005 Disney Enterprises, Inc. All rights reserved under International and Pan-American Copyright Conventions.
Published in the United States by Random House Children's Books, a division of Random House, Inc., New York, NY 10019,
and simultaneously in Canada by Random House of Canada Limited, Toronto, in conjunction with Disney Enterprises, Inc.
RANDOM HOUSE and colophon are registered trademarks of Random House, Inc.
Manufactured for Random House by Phidal Publishing, Inc.
ISBN: 0-7364-2355-9
www.randomhouse.com/kids/disney
MANUFACTURED IN CHINA
10 9 8 7 6 5 4 3 2

The Castle Grounds

Cinderella loves walking through the castle grounds.
Use your stickers to fill in the scene.

A New Dress

Making a pretty new dress is fun.
Use your stickers to help Cinderella add the finishing touches.

Friends and Family

Cinderella likes to keep pictures of her friends and family in pretty frames.
Use your stickers to put each of them in the right frame.

The Royal Rose Garden

Cinderella wants to pick some fresh flowers before the ball.
Use your stickers to decorate the scene.

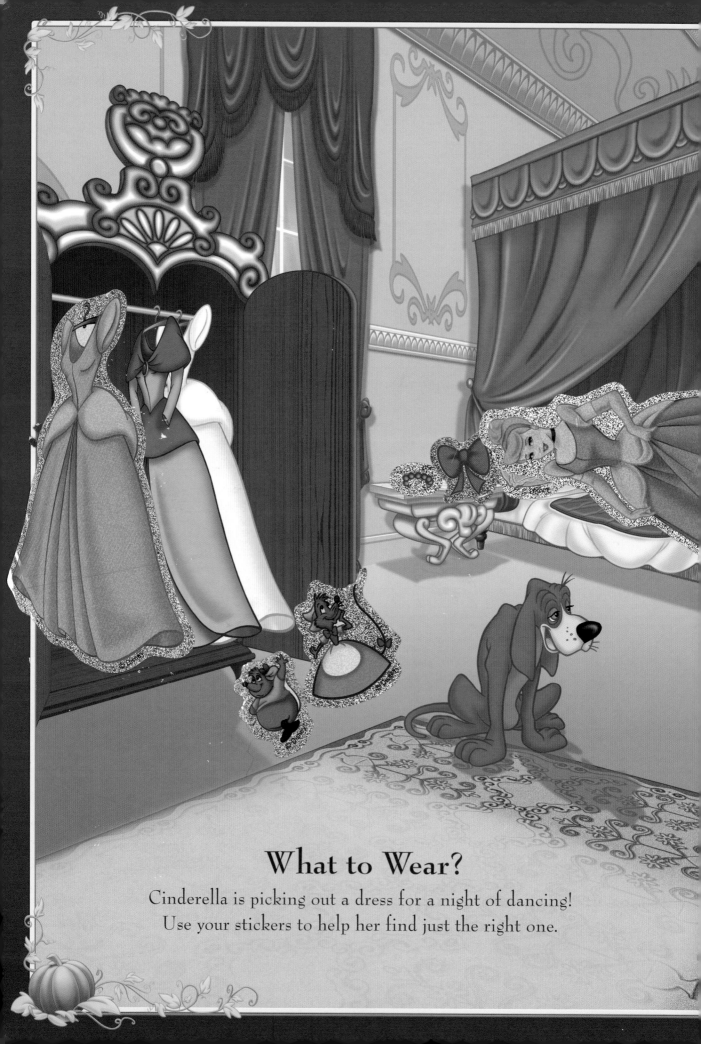

What to Wear?

Cinderella is picking out a dress for a night of dancing!
Use your stickers to help her find just the right one.

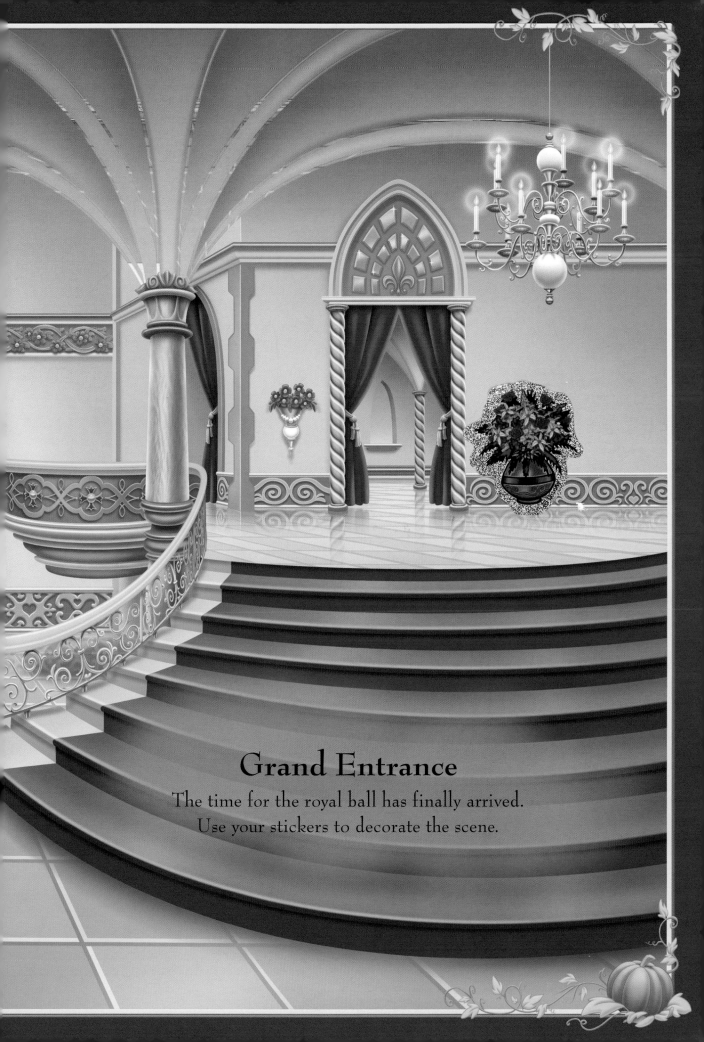

Grand Entrance

The time for the royal ball has finally arrived.
Use your stickers to decorate the scene.

Another Happy Ending

After the ball, Cinderella and the Prince ride away in the royal carriage.
Use your stickers to decorate the scene.